I DREAM OF A MAN FLYING through the air, carrying a basket of fruit — apples and peaches, cherries and grapes, pears and plums, but he give me a mango.

A breakfast smell wake me out of bed and pull
me to the kitchen.
"Good morning, Malaika," Mummy say.
"I had a dream," I say.
Grandma stop mixing the dough. "Go on."

When I tell them about the man
with the basket of fruit, Mummy
leave the kitchen. Grandma tell
Adèle and me to go play outside.

We play carnival and tag. We jump
rope. We even eat snacks.
"Can we come inside now?" I ask.
"*Nous sommes fatiguées,*" Adèle say.
Papa Fred ask, "Who wants to make
pizza? *Et regarde un film?*"

Of course, we say yes.
We even have a dance
party. But something
don't feel right.

After dinner, Mummy say she have something to tell me about my dream.

"Was that my daddy?" I ask.

Mummy say yes, and she tell me about him. When I was a baby, my daddy came to Canada before us to work on a farm. He picked fruit and sent the money back home to help Grandma, Mummy and me. But one day he got very sick and passed away.

I want to fly away to see my daddy, fly like he did in my dream.

"Chile, I have something for you," Grandma say. She give me a letter.

I take out a picture of a man with a big smile holding a basket of fruit. Just like in my dream.

"To Malaika, my likkle one," the words on the back say.

"Did he love me?" I ask Mummy.

"Yes, darling. Very, very much."

"I think it's time we take you to know more about your daddy," Grandma say.

One day, we all take a long, long trip. We go on
highways, over bridges, beside water. The car stop.
We eat and go to the bathroom, then we're off again.

We pass green and gold fields — wide, meeting the sky — and cows and horses eating. The car stop again, this time at a farm.

"Good afternoon," a man say.

He's wearing overalls, just like my daddy, and he talk like us too.

"I'm Mr. Easton. Your father was my friend, like my brother. He tell me about his little angel Malaika. Do you want to see where your daddy used to work?"

My heart grow big.

"Yes," I say.

Mr. Easton show me the trees where Daddy
picked fruit.
He show me the tractor my daddy used to drive.
Then Mr. Easton take us to meet some of
Daddy's friends.

"Your father had a big, big dream," one say.
"To have a carnival here, like back home."
"To bring everyone together."
"A parade ..."
"With lots of music."

"My daddy was just like me," I say.

"It'd be an honor if you be the Carnival Queen and march with us at the harvest festival," Mr. Easton say.

"What do you think?" Grandma ask me.

"Yes, please!"

Everyone cheer.

My cheeks hurt from smiling on
the long drive all the way home.
When I go to sleep, I have another
dream, an idea for the parade.

"Let's make signs!" I say to Adèle the next day.

We make colorful posters. We put them up in our neighborhood.

First, Tante Josée and Oncle Claude bring me a blue cloth with four white *fleurs-de-lis*.

Luc Laveau bring me cloth from Wendake.

Some of our neighbors bring different colors of cloth — some are shiny, others are soft.

Grandma add some of her cloth from back home.

Malayka M. bring me something special from Somalia.

"For you," she say.

Grandma and I stitch together the biggest, most
colorful carnival flag.

Mummy pack bags of snacks to share with the farm
workers — plantain chips and small packs of cookies.

Early the next morning, we get up for the long drive back
to the farm.

Grandma and Mummy help me into my carnival peacock
dress. Two of the workers braid my hair and do my makeup.

I wish my daddy could see me now.

"*Une vraie reine*. I am so proud of you," Papa Fred say.

"Malaika, can you count us in?"
Mr. Easton ask.
    I nod, and in a very loud voice I say,
"Ready? 3 ... 2 ... 1 ... GO!"

We dance and bounce and march down the road and through the town, to soca and reggae music. I hold the great big carnival flag, full of the people I love, my family close behind.

I feel like I'm flying.

AUTHOR'S NOTE

Malaika's father was a seasonal agricultural or farm worker, a type of migrant worker. When Malaika was still a baby, he left for Canada to pick fruit on a farm, like thousands of other migrant workers who are mostly from Mexico and Jamaica, but from other Caribbean countries and parts of the world as well.

Migrant workers are very important. The farms where they work depend on them, and they, in turn, can send money home to support their families. Despite their importance, these workers face many challenges. They often live in crowded housing, and they are not always made to feel like they belong in the communities where they work and live for eight months a year, or sometimes longer. They are far from their friends and family back home and work long days.

Both of my grandfathers were seasonal farm workers in the United States. Sadly, one of them passed away before he could return home to Jamaica to see his family, and so I didn't get a chance to meet him. *Malaika, Carnival Queen* was inspired by him.